MAMA, LET'S MAKE A MOON

by
CLAY RICE

Mama, Let's Make A Moon

Published by Familius LLC, Huntsville, Utah, www.familius.com

Familius books are available at special discounts for bulk purchases for sales promotions, family or corporate use. Special editions, including personalized covers, excerpts of existing books, or books with corporate logos, can be created in large quantities for special needs. For more information, contact Premium Sales at 801-552-7298 or email specialmarkets@familius.com

Edited by Pete Wyrick
Book and jacket design by Steve Lepre
Clay Rice bio photograph by Debbie Jones

Printed in China

LCCN: 2012945115

eISBN: 978-1-938301-05-6
pISBN: 978-1-938301-06-3

First Edition

About the Publisher

Familius was founded in 2012 with the intent to align the founders' love of publishing and family with the digital publishing renaissance which occurred simultaneously with the Great Recession. The founders believe that the traditional family is the basic unit of society, and that a society is only as strong as the families that create it.

Familius' mission is to help families be happy. We invite you to participate with us in strengthening your family by being part of the Familius family. Go to www.familius. com to subscribe and receive information about our books, articles, and videos.

Website: www.familius.com
Facebook:www.facebook.com/paterfamilius
Twitter: @paterfamilius1 and @familiustalk
Pinterest: www.pinterest.com/familius

HELPING FAMILIES BE HAPPY

DEDICATION

These torn-edged silhouettes,
rustic, yet highly detailed, rose from
the fertile mountain soil of my wife's raisin'.

To me, like she, they are as sweet as sassafras
and as comforting as wood smoke,
or old folks playing checkers.

The sweetness and strength of Mama,
the laughter of children,
the homegrown sense of place; it's all in here.

This one's for you Mama.

Mama, let's make a moon,
the little girl sighed,
as tall as the mountains,
as wide as the sky.

Mama, let's make a moon, it won't cost too much;
we'll use secondhand stardust, and leftover love.

BOX
O'
SILLY!

We'll stuff it with silly,

and marshmallow goo

AUNT SALLIE'S
MARSHMALLOW
GOO

and paint it with promise;
Mama, let's make a moon.

Mama pulled from the cupboard
a weathered old box,
handmade and fastened
with curlicue locks.

The children chose partners...

joy filled the room,

Mama opened an envelope...

Recipe for a Moon

Recipe For A Moon
A streamful of silver
A white Swan's Starry Shi...
2 Possums Paws of
Dreamdust from the
Imagination Mine

RECIPE FOR A MOON

A stream full of silver,

a swan's starry shine,

three jars full of fireflies,

some marshmallow goo,

a dipper of dew,

and milk of moo.

Mix these together
in the old miners cart
with a stout canoe paddle,
and love from your heart.

So they made a BIG moon
as wide as the sky;
as tall as the mountains,
bright as a firefly.

They pushed it and rolled it
with all of their will;
forest creatures joined in
as they moved up the hill.

Let's hang the moon, Mama!
the children both shrieked;
deer danced with approval,
bear lumbered toward the peak.

With the fox from the holler
and the mouse from the mill,
they climbed the big tree
at the top of the hill.

A thrust from the deer,
a shove from the bear,
hands, paws, and antlers
high in the air.

They climbed through the sky
and with light from above,
hung in the heavens,
from star steps of love

a silvery, shiny,
(slightly stickery) lune;
the stars are all smiling;
Mama, we hung the moon!

ACKNOWLEDGEMENTS:

Many thanks to Caroline Rice, Charlie Rice, and Connor Rice,
Claire Nelson, Elisabeth Nelson, and Carter Nelson, Whit
& Jazzy for their time and effort in making this project.
To Steve Lepre, for his talent and patience
in the lengthy process of designing this book.
And to Jack Alterman for his skill and talent.

To Katherine Rice, whose faith in my dream never wavered,
even as mine did, and to all the Mamas across this great country,
who teach their children what is really important.

Clay's work can be seen online at: www.clayrice.com